DISNEY'S
EASY-TO-READ

To School and Beyond

A collection
of 6 new
exciting stories

A
MOUSE WORKS
STORYBOOK COLLECTION

"Beauty and the Beast: Chip's Favorite Season" is based on the original
story Beauty and the Beast: Chip's Favorite Season, illustrated by Sol Studios.

"A Bug's Life: Flik's Perfect Gift" is based on the original story A Bug's Life: Flik's
Perfect Gift, illustrated by Pulsar Studios, Scott Tilley, and Andrea and John Alvin.

"Pocahontas: Where's Flit?" is based on the original story
Pocahontas: Where's Flit?, illustrated by Eric Binder and Darren Hont.

"Aladdin: Genie School" is based on the original story
Aladdin: Genie School, illustrated by Christian Monte and Adam Devaney.

"The Lion King: Simba's Pouncing Lesson" is based on the original
story The Lion King: Simba's Pouncing Lesson, illustrated by Sol Studios.

"Toy Story: To School and Beyond" is based on the original
story Toy Story: To School — And Beyond!, illustrated by Sol Studios.

CONTENTS

Chip's Favorite Season

Patrick Daley

It's here! It's here!

Today is the day.

What will we tell him?

What will we say?

Wake up, Chip.
It's time to play.
Winter is here.
What do
you say?

Slide down the hill.

Skate on the ice.

I like winter.

It's so nice!

Wake up, Chip.

It's time to play.

Spring is here.

What do you say?

Jump in the mud.

Make a mess.

I like spring.

It's the best!

Wake up, Chip.

It's time to play.

Summer is here.

What do you say?

Swim in the pond.

Play in the sun.

I like summer.

It's so much fun!

Wake up, Chip.

It's time to play.

Fall is here.

What do you say?

Rake all the leaves.

Jump in the pile.

I like fall.

It makes me smile.

Winter
Spring
Summer
Fall.

Chip likes the seasons.

He likes them all.

Flik's Perfect Gift

Judy Katschke

It is Queen Atta's
birthday.

All the ants are
bringing gifts!

But what's bugging Flik?

"I want to bring
the perfect gift!"
Flik said.

Flik looked high.

Flik looked low.

Finding the perfect
gift is no picnic!

Flik thought
and thought.

"I've got it!"
he cried.

Flik's ideas
started to bloom!

"It's just a plain
old daisy now,"
Flik said to Dot.

"But soon it will be . . .

a merry-go-round for Atta!

Come on, Dot,

let's try it out!"

WHOOPS!

"Maybe Atta can use

a nice, cool breeze!

Get ready to

CHILL, Dot!"

WHOOSH!

"Or how about a new
way for Atta to fly?

Hop on, Dot!"

WHOAA!

"Maybe you should just get Atta a card," Dot said.

"No," Flik cried.

"I *will* find the perfect present!"

"I will build her a beach umbrella!" Flik said.
"A sprinkler!
A Ferris wheel!"

Uh-oh. It's Queen Atta!

"What's that, Flik?"

Queen Atta asked.

"It's just a plain old daisy," Flik said.

"It's perfect," Queen Atta cried.

"It is?" Flik asked.

He looked at the

daisy and smiled.

"IT IS!

Happy

birthday, Atta!"

Where's Flit?

Bettina Ling

"Let's go see
Grandmother Willow,"
Pocahontas called to
Flit and Meeko.
"There is the path.
Come on, let's go."

As Meeko led the way,
Pocahontas stopped to say,
"Where's Flit?"

Here's a
good place to hide.
Pocahontas
looked inside.

No Flit.

Pocahontas
looked in a tree.
What's up there?
Whose nest did
she see?

Not Flit's.

Meeko heard a sound.

He looked all around.

Still no Flit.

Is Flit down a hole?

Or inside the log?

Or is he in the mud

with a tiny frog?

Where else can they look?

Where else can they go?

Maybe Grandmother

Willow will know.

Pocahontas said, "Where's Flit?"

Look who they see in the old willow tree.

It's Flit!

Abu handed Aladdin
the empty plate.

"Thanks, Abu,"
Aladdin said.
"You are more fun
than a barrel of monkeys."

Genie
snapped his
fingers.
A big barrel
appeared.

Monkeys popped out
of the barrel and began
to sing and dance.

Abu did not join in.

The monkeys took

a bow. In a flash, the

barrel was

gone.

"Where did you learn
that trick?"
asked Jasmine.

"In genie school,"
said Genie.
"Close your eyes and
I'll take you."

He snapped his fingers
and said, "KA-ZAM!"

Aladdin and Jasmine were sitting in a very strange classroom.

There were yellow genies, red genies, purple genies, and even a teeny-weeny green genie.

"Good morning, class," said Genie.
"Today we are going to talk about
appearing and . . ."

But before Genie could say
"disappearing," all the genies
disappeared!

A moment later they
came back.

"Bravo! Bravo!"
Genie said proudly.

"I guess he wasn't kidding
about genie school,"
Jasmine said to Aladdin.

A nanny goat and

her three kids appeared.

They erased the chalk-

board with their tails.

When it was clean,

Genie made the

goats disappear.

"Now, let's do some math," said Genie.

"Math!" groaned the teeny-weeny green genie. "Who needs math?"

"We give out three wishes," said Genie. "No more, no less."

"If you do not learn your numbers, your work would never be done," Genie said.

"Now, count along with me," said Genie.

"One . . . Two . . . Three!"

When their math lesson was over, the little genies had some milk and cookies.

"I also know a few tricks," Aladdin said.

He ate his third cookie.

"Really?" Jasmine said. "Show me."

"You just saw one,"
said Aladdin.
"I made three yummy
cookies disappear."

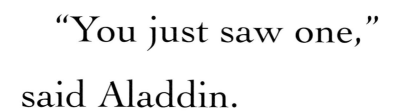

"That is your trick?"
Jasmine said.

"I can top that.
I can grow a mustache."

Jasmine drank a glass
of milk.

"KA-ZAM!" she said.

After snacks, it was
time for a nap.
All of the genies
disappeared into
their lamps.

When the genies woke
up, they were ready to
learn their ABCs.

"A is for apple,"
said a red genie.

He snapped his fingers.

An apple

appeared on

his desk.

"B is for banana,"
a yellow genie said.

She snapped her
fingers and a banana
appeared.

At three o'clock, the
bell rang.

"School's out!"
cried Genie.

The yellow genies got on yellow carpets.

The red genies got on red carpets.

The purple genies got on purple magic carpets, and the teeny-weeny green genie got on his teeny-weeny green carpet.

"How will we get
home?" asked Aladdin.

"We don't have a magic
flying carpet,"
said Jasmine.

"KA-ZAM!" cried
Genie.

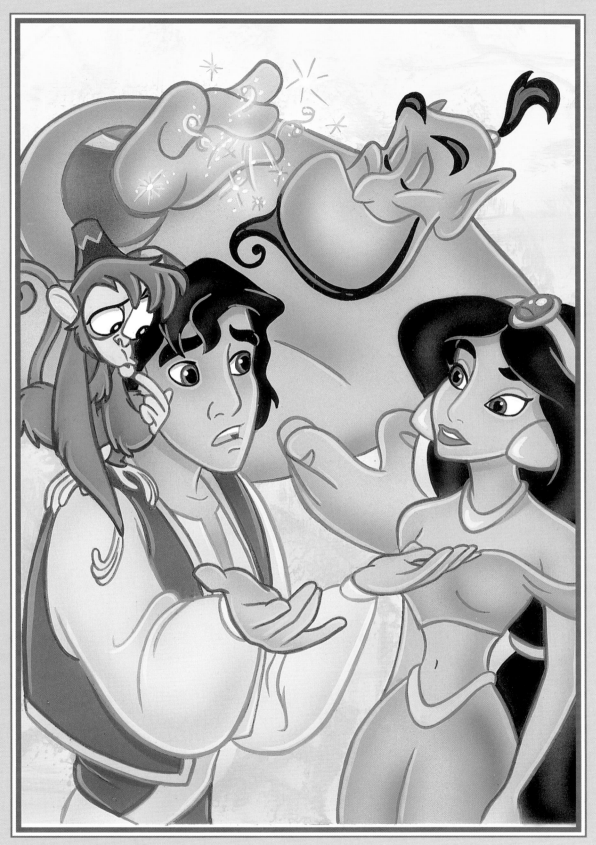

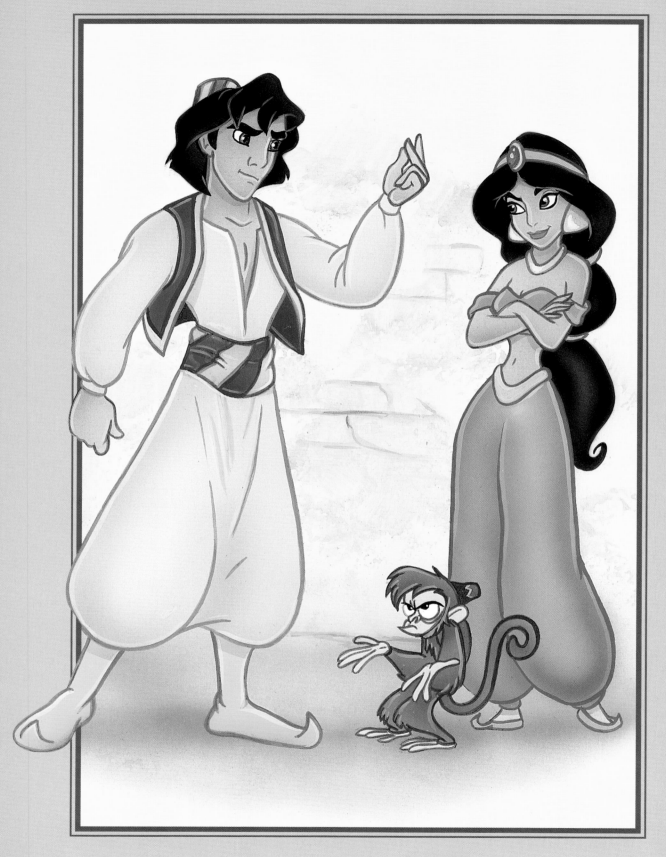

Back in Agrabah,
Aladdin wanted to try
some tricks.

"Get ready, Abu,"
said Aladdin.

"B is for banana!"
Aladdin snapped his
fingers.

Nothing happened.

Genie appeared.

He handed Abu a bunch

of bananas.

"Why can't I do

that?" said

Aladdin.

"I went

to genie

school."

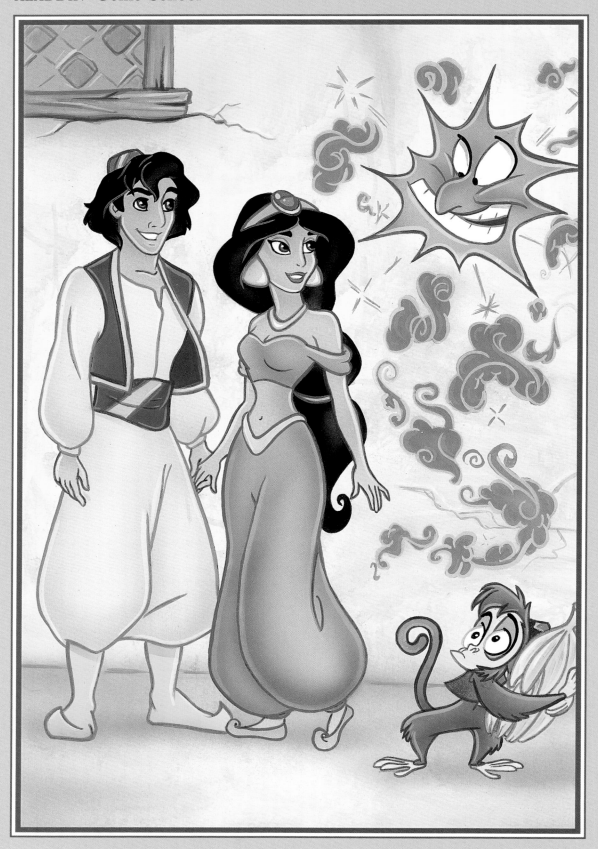

"Al, my pal," said Genie, "appearing and disappearing is for genies only."

And Genie waved good-bye . . .

. . . and disappeared!

THE
LION KING

Simba's
Pouncing Lesson

Gail Tuchman

In the jungle
of monkeys and trees,
and swinging vines,
and a cooling breeze,
came a cry from Timon.
"Eeeeee-yaaaa!
Charge . . . Pumbaa!"

"What are you doing, kid?" Pumbaa asked.

"Pouncing," said Simba, "but I missed."

"Timon," said Pumbaa. "Let's help our cub. He needs a lesson in getting some grub."

"Here's how to pounce,"
Timon pointed out,
as he tiptoed about
on Pumbaa's snout.
"First, tiptoe,
nice and slow.
Then, pounce.
Ready, set, GO!"

"Okay," said Simba.
"I will give it a shake.
Watch me pounce
on that big snake."

Simba said to himself,
First, tiptoe, nice and slow.
Then, pounce.

Ready, set,

GO!

In the jungle of
monkeys and trees,
and swinging vines,
and a cooling breeze,
Simba missed.

The snake hissed.

"This time,"
said Pumbaa,
"pretend you are a spy
and follow that fly.
Creep close,
then leap high."

"Okay," said Simba.
"I will give it a try.
"I will pretend
I'm a spy
and follow that fly.
Creep close,
then leap high."

In the jungle
of monkeys and trees,
and swinging vines,
and a cooling breeze,
Simba SNEEZED.

The fly flew away.

He was pleased.

"Try again, kid,"
Timon called out,
as he bounced about
on Pumbaa's snout.
"It's the bounce
that counts
when you want
to pounce!"

Simba thought
of what his father had said.
"Stay low to the ground,
and don't make a sound."

So Simba quietly
practiced
pouncing
around.

Pumbaa and Timon
were sniffing for ants.
Simba hid and
watched from behind
some plants.

The lion cub stayed
low to the ground,
and without making
a sound . . .

. . . Simba pounced.

"GOTCHA!" he proudly

announced.

"Good surprise, kid,"

said Pumbaa with a groan.

"Great pouncing," moaned Timon.

In the jungle
of monkeys and trees,
and swinging vines,
and a cooling breeze,
came a cry.

"Eeeeee-yaaaa!
HOORAY . . . Simba!"

To School
and Beyond

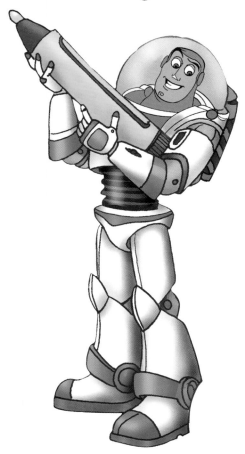

Judy Katschke

"What is Andy doing?"
Buzz asked.

"It's the 100th day of
school," said Woody.

"Andy is bringing in 100
toys for show-and-tell."

The toys were happy that Buzz and
Woody were chosen to go to school.

"You have been chosen!"

the alien said.

"School sounds like a strange planet," Buzz said. "What if I do not like it there?"

"You will," Woody said.

Sarge got his troops marching.

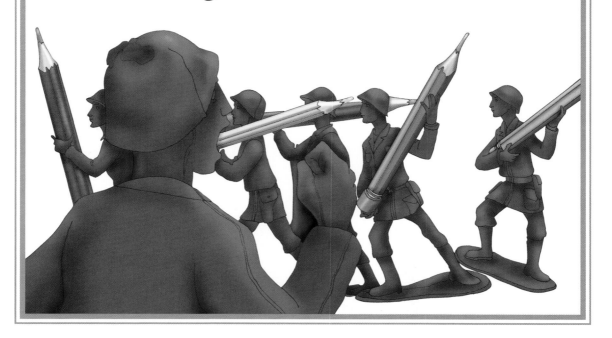

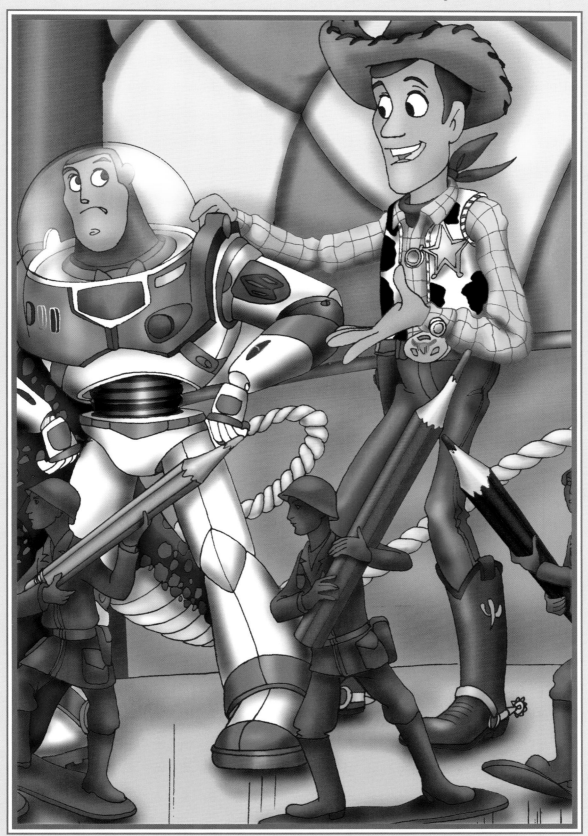

At school Andy put his backpack in his cubby.

Buzz and Woody peeked out of the backpack.

Buzz hopped out.

"I think I will like it here," Buzz said.

Woody ran after Buzz.

"Get back in that pack!" Woody said.

"Andy needs us for show-and-tell!"

Buzz ran down the hall. Woody followed him.

Buzz looked into a classroom.

"No, Buzz," Woody said. "That is not Andy's class."

"It is kindergarten!"

Kindergarten means finger paints!

Sticky fingers grabbed

Buzz and Woody.

"We have to find Buzz and Woody!" Sarge said. "Let's go to the mess hall!"

A cook saw Sarge and his men.

"Green ants!" she yelled.

She grabbed a big can of bug spray.

"Run for cover!" Sarge yelled.

Buzz and Woody
escaped from kindergarten,
but Buzz saw something
else.

BUZZZZZZZZZZ!

BUZZZZZZZ!

"This robot knows
my name!"
Buzz said.

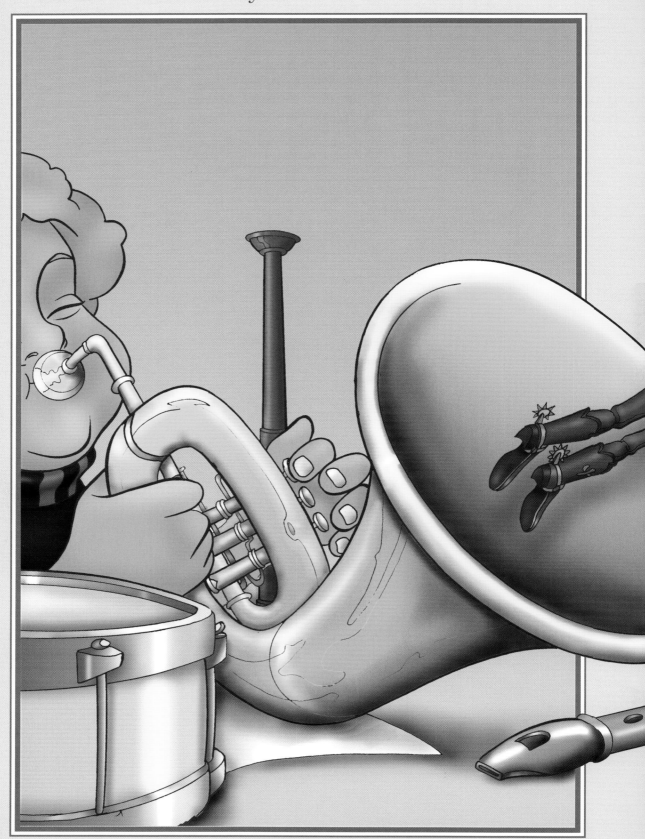

"We have
to hurry,"
said Woody.
But Buzz ran
into the music room.
"This place is fun!"
Buzz yelled.
Buzz and Woody
were blasted out of
a trumpet.

"Let's move, move, move!" Sarge yelled. But, the green army men were stuck in glue. Sarge was not happy. Finding Buzz and Woody was not easy!

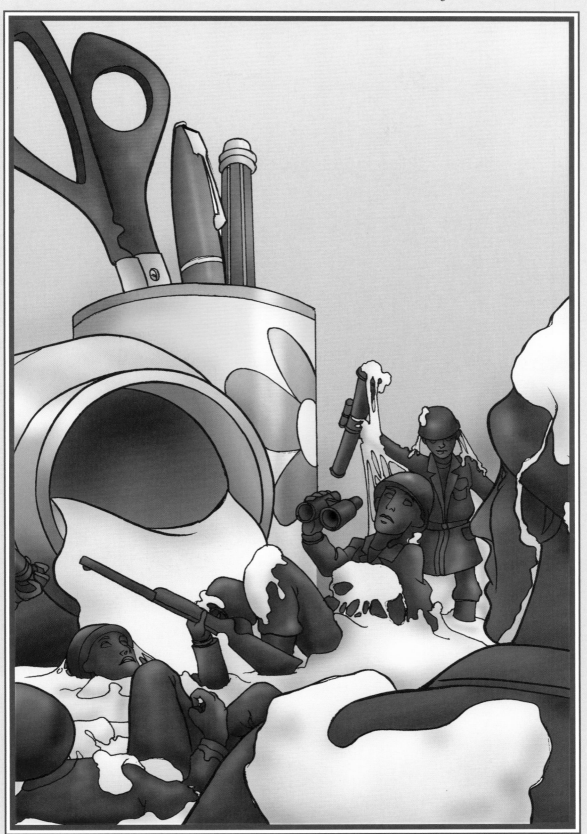

"We are in a crater," Buzz said.

"It is a water hole!" Woody said.

"Crater!"

"Water hole!"

Water shot out at Buzz.

"You are right, Woody," said Buzz.

"We have to find Andy's cubby," said Woody.

Too late!

A boy grabbed him.

Another boy grabbed Buzz.

"Mine," one boy said.

"No, it's mine," said the other boy.

Buzz and Woody were happy when a teacher stepped in.

"These toys belong to ME now!" she said.

The teacher threw them into her

drawer. They were not alone.

"No toy has escaped this
drawer!" a doll said.

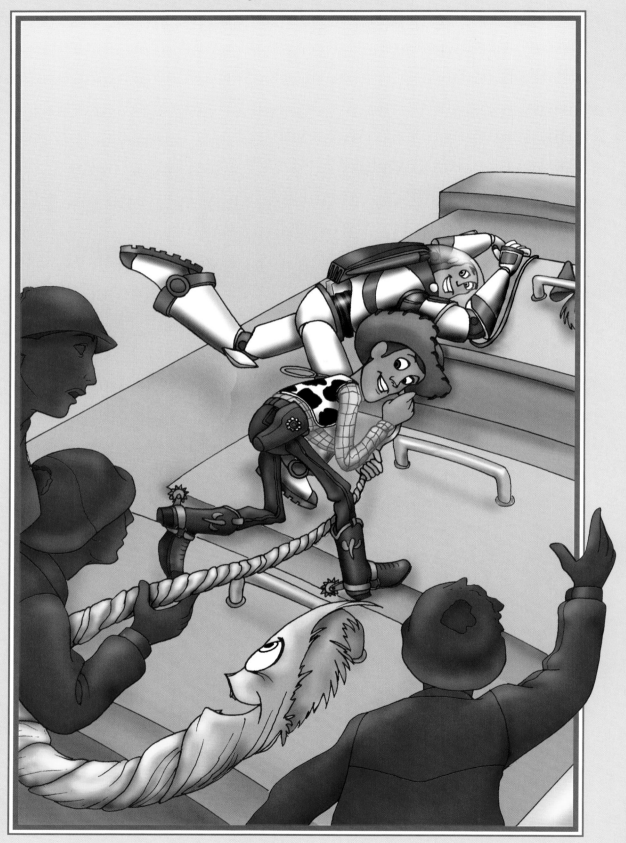

"Now we will really miss show-and-tell!" Woody said.

"Not true, Lawman!" yelled Sarge.

The green army men pushed the drawer open.

Buzz and Woody were free!

The toys made it back
to Andy's cubby just in
time.

"I have 100 toys for
show-and-tell," said Andy.

Buzz and Woody
smiled.